SOCCER MACHINE

By Dusti Bowling

For Younger Readers

AVEN GREEN SLEUTHING MACHINE

AVEN GREEN BAKING MACHINE

AVEN GREEN MUSIC MACHINE

AVEN GREEN SOCCER MACHINE

For Older Readers

INSIGNIFICANT EVENTS IN THE LIFE OF A CACTUS

24 HOURS IN NOWHERE

MOMENTOUS EVENTS IN THE LIFE OF A CACTUS

THE CANYON'S EDGE

ACROSS THE DESERT

SOCCER MACHINE

DUSTI BOWLING
illustrated by GINA PERRY

union
square
kids

NEW YORK

union square kids

NEW YORK

UNION SQUARE KIDS and the distinctive Union Square Kids logo are trademarks
of Union Square & Co., LLC.

Union Square & Co., LLC, is a subsidiary of Sterling Publishing Co., Inc.

Text © 2023 Dusti Bowling
Interior illustrations © 2023 Gina Perry
Cover art © 2023 Union Square & Co., LLC

ISBN 978-1-4549-4223-8 (hardcover)
ISBN 978-1-4549-4183-5 (paperback)
ISBN 978-1-4549-4187-3 (e-book)

Library of Congress Control Number: 2022031691

For information about custom editions, special sales, and premium purchases, please contact
specialsales@unionsquareandco.com.

Printed in Canada
Lot #:
2 4 6 8 10 9 7 5 3 1
02/23

unionsquareandco.com

Cover illustration by Marta Kissi
Cover and interior design by Whitney Manger and Julie Robine

For my own Soccer Machine, Adlai

Contents

Chapter 1

The Best Soccer Player
I Know

Kids play a lot of different sports in elementary school: baseball, softball, basketball, dodgeball, Simon Says, and Butts Up. But the best of all sports is the one I like to play, and that sport is called soccer!

I'm already the best soccer player I know, even though I only just started last year in second grade. And I don't play soccer like everyone else. Actually, wait a minute. Yes, I do! Everyone has to use their feet to play soccer, and so do I. Because you see, I don't have arms. Yep, you heard me. No arms here on my torso, which I'd like to add is already eight years old.

That means when I kick the soccer ball, I use my feet. And when I do a knee trap, I use my knee. And when I chest the soccer ball, I use my chest. And when I headbutt the soccer ball, I use my butt. Just joking. I use my head, of course. I only use my butt during some of my best soccer moves, like my top secret booty trap. And everyone knows about the toot decoy.

Dad was the one who got me really interested in soccer. One day he brought home a soccer ball from the store, and we just started kicking it around the yard. Then he built a soccer goal out of some plumbing pipes and a fishnet. Every time I kicked the ball into the homemade goal, it would fall to pieces, which was so much fun, even if Dad didn't think so. Then Dad bought a *real* soccer goal that didn't fall to pieces.

Dad said soccer and I were made for each other, and he's totally right! Soccer is probably my second most favorite thing to do, right after eating gummy bears and mint chocolate chip ice cream. Dad was my coach last year, and this year he's going to be my coach again. And guess what? Emily and Kayla are on my team too. They're pretty good at soccer, but they're not as good as I am. Because they don't know how to do the top secret booty trap.

Chapter 2

No More Mister Nice Sujata

My friends and I practiced our best soccer moves outside at recess. "I can't wait for soccer to start!" I shouted as I kicked the ball to Kayla.

"This is going to be the best season ever!" Kayla cried as she headbutted the ball to Emily.

The ball bounced off Emily's unibrow, and she kneed it back to me. "We're going to kick everyone else's butts," she said, rubbing her forehead.

Sujata stood nearby, watching us quietly and looking a little left out. "You want to play, too, Sujata?" I asked her.

Her face lit up, and she ran over. "Those aren't very good soccer shoes," I told her, pointing down at her beautiful gold sandals. "You could hurt your toes."

Sujata looked sad as she began to turn away. "Okay," she said softly.

"But you know what," said Kayla. "If we don't kick the ball too hard, I think it will be okay."

"That's a great idea, Kayla!" I declared. Even though my best kicks were extra powerful, I was also good at soft kicking. And medium kicking.

Sujata smiled and joined our circle, and we all kicked the ball around very gently so that Sujata wouldn't hurt her bare toes. Because that's what friends are for.

"You know," said Kayla, "some of the players on our team had to quit."

"Why?" asked Sujata.

"One girl moved away to Texas," said Kayla.

"And another girl decided she liked tap dancing a lot more, and her parents will only let her do one after-school activity," I said.

"So I'm thinking you should maybe join our team," said Kayla.

"It's lots of fun," said Emily. "We even have ice cream parties."

Sujata's brown eyes got all big, like ice cream parties were the most exciting things she'd ever heard of. She was right. "Do you think I could be good enough?" she asked.

"Well," I said, looking down at her gold sandals. "You'll need new shoes."

Sujata nodded quickly. "Yes, I can get new shoes."

"And you'll need a uniform," said Emily.

"And you'll need to practice really hard," added Kayla.

Sujata nodded again. "I can practice really hard."

"And you have to get tough," I said. "Don't be afraid to steal the ball from another player.

7

You just go ahead and do *flip-flaps* all around the other team and kick that ball as hard as you can at the goalie. No more Mister Nice Sujata!"

Sujata's eyes got even bigger and she gulped. "I'll try," she said softly.

"But you also have to be nice to everyone all the time," I said much more calmly. "Got it?"

Sujata nodded. "Got it," she said. "Except what's a flip-flap?"

"It's like when you *feint*," I said.

Sujata's mouth dropped open. "Like this?" she asked, closing her eyes and dropping to the ground.

"No, not like that!" I cried, and we all giggled. "It's when you fake a move!"

Sujata stood up and gave us a sheepish look. "Sorry," she said.

"That's okay," said Kayla, hopping from foot to foot all excitedly. She was really good at the flip-flap. "It's a great soccer move," she said, grabbing the soccer ball with her toes and dribbling it toward Sujata. "You make it look like you're going to go one way. And then— surprise!" Kayla changed direction around Sujata. "You actually go another way." Kayla stopped with her foot on the soccer ball and faced Sujata. "I'll teach you how to do it."

Sujata smiled and folded her hands together in front of her excited face. "I can't wait," she said. Then we taught Sujata our special huddle and hand-and-foot-stack cheer we always did before every practice and game. She would need to learn it if she was going to be a part of our team. She was going to need to learn a lot, but lucky for her, we were good teachers and Dad was a good coach. I couldn't wait for Sujata to join our team!

Chapter 3

Cap'n Aven

The first day of soccer practice finally arrived, and I couldn't have been more excited. Mom helped me put on all my super special gear. I had brand-new *cleats* with Velcro so I could put them on and take them off more easily. I also had shin guards to protect my *shins*. Your shin is a chunk of your leg that gets kicked sometimes in soccer. It's not the same thing as your chin, which is a chunk of your face.

And, of course, I had my special team uniform, which had my own name and number on the back: Green 8. It was perfect because I was also eight years old! On the front was our team name, which Dad had let us pick out ourselves: The Sticker Kickers. It was a good name because we all liked stickers. And we also liked kicking. But none of us actually liked kicking stickers. That was okay, though. It was still the best team name ever.

Dad and I drove to the field together, and he put on his special "Getting Pumped for Soccer" playlist in the car. We opened the windows and sang as loud as we could along

with "We Will Rock You" until we reached the park, where some of my teammates were already waiting for us.

"Hi!" said this girl Lexi. She was pretty nice, even if she always had snot dripping out of her nose. Dad said Lexi had allergies, and she was allergic to the grass on the field, so I tried to be very understanding about the snot situation.

Then I saw Emily and Kayla, and we all three jumped up and hugged because the first day of soccer practice was one of the most

exciting days of the whole year! Then guess what happened? Sujata showed up! And she had on a team uniform and shin guards and good shoes that weren't sandals and everything. Our three-person hug turned into an even happier four-person hug.

"Listen up, ladies!" said Coach Dad, clapping his hands, and we all gathered around. "Who's excited for our first practice?"

We all jumped up and down and screamed, and I performed a magnificent kick in the air, which came very close to Lexi's face by accident.

"This is going to be a very special season," said Coach Dad. "I can tell by looking around at all of you talented people." He eyed each of us one by one, like he could truly see our soccer talents. "And I'm so excited to welcome some new girls to the team."

Then Coach Dad called up one of the new girls. "This is Ana," said Coach Dad. "Everyone welcome Ana to the team."

"Welcome, Ana!" I shouted loud enough to knock the blades of grass down. At least that's what Coach Dad said, but I think he was just joking because the grass was still standing straight up.

Then Coach Dad called up Sujata. Emily, Kayla, and I all jumped up and down excitedly and were already shouting "Welcome, Sujata!" before Coach Dad even had a chance to introduce her to the rest of the team.

"This is going to be a very special season," said Coach Dad. "Because this year, I've decided you've all gotten old enough and mature enough to have a soccer captain."

Lexi raised her hand and asked, "What's *mature* mean?"

"It means you wear a bra," said another girl on the team named Stacy. "Like my older sister. She's mature."

All of us gasped and looked around at one another, hardly believing that any of us could be wearing a bra. And why did we need to be wearing bras to have a soccer captain anyway?

Coach Dad closed his eyes and rubbed his forehead. "No, no that's not what it means," he said, sighing. Then he looked at all of us, but we were all too busy looking at one another to see if anyone's bra straps were sticking out of their jerseys.

"Listen," said Coach Dad, picking up the soccer ball at his feet and twisting it around in his hands. "Being mature means you act grown-up in certain ways. For example, when you lose a game, you smile and shake hands with the winning team. And when you make a mistake, you apologize. You also encourage and support your team members."

Emily let out a big breath. "Boy, that sounds like *a lot*," she said.

Coach Dad nodded, still holding the soccer ball. "Yes, but I know you can do it. And that's why I think you're ready for a team captain."

"What's the captain do?" asked Lexi, sniffling and rubbing at her snot. "Is it like a ship captain?"

"Is it like Cap'n Crunch?" asked Stacy. "That's my favorite cereal."

"Is it like Captain America?" asked Emily.

"Does the captain get to wear a special costume?" asked Ana.

Coach Dad looked a little confused for a moment, like he'd forgotten what a captain even was. Then he started shaking his head.

"No, no ships or cereal or costumes," he said. "The captain wears the same jersey as the rest of us."

"Can we still call them Cap'n?" I asked. Because "Cap'n Aven" had a really nice ring to it.

"That's fine," said Coach Dad, now tossing the soccer ball from one hand to the other. "The important thing isn't what she's called. The important thing is what she does. The captain has to behave like a leader. It's a big responsibility. The captain represents our team. She has to guide and support and encourage her teammates."

"Piece of cake," I declared, and I definitely would've snapped my fingers if I had any.

"How are you going to choose the captain?" asked Kayla.

"Good question, Kayla," said Coach Dad. "I'm going to watch how you girls behave and work together during the next few practices. Then I'll decide based on your *sportsmanship*."

"I thought you said it had nothing to do with ships," said Lexi.

"Sportsmanship doesn't have anything to do with ships," said Coach Dad.

"But it really sounds like a man driving a ship," said Lexi, wiping her nose.

"Sportsmanship is how you behave while you're playing soccer," said Coach Dad. "It's about being kind and fair and doing your best. Got it?"

We all nodded our heads, and I looked around at my teammates with a big fat smirk on my face. If sportsmanship was about whoever did the best, then they didn't stand a chance against me, because I was definitely the best player on the field.

Watch out, team! Cap'n Aven's in charge now!

Chapter 4

Lots of Winking

We had Great-grandma over for dinner that night after practice was done. Mom made a special dinner of spaghetti and meatballs, which she called spaghetti and soccer balls, even though the "soccer balls" still just looked like regular old meatballs. Great-grandma brought her tomato soup cake. She'd made it extra special, too, by putting a great big soccer ball made out of frosting on top.

"How did your first practice go?" asked Great-grandma, taking a bite of spaghetti.

Smitty, Great-grandma's dog, sat under the table, waiting for a dropped noodle. He knew the best spot was near my seat.

"It was great," I said, dropping a noodle down to Smitty, who gobbled it up in one bite. "Dad has decided to make one of us the soccer captain this year, and I wonder who it's going to be." I winked at Dad.

Dad smiled, spaghetti sauce at the corners of his mouth. "It could be anyone, Aven," he said. "It depends on how the next few practices go."

I winked at him again. "Suuuure," I said. "It could be anyone. Anyone at all." I winked some more.

"Do you have spaghetti sauce in your eye, honey?" asked Great-grandma.

"No," I said. "Dad and I just have an . . . understanding."

Dad shook his head. "Seriously, Aven," he said. "I don't know who the soccer captain will be yet."

"I gotcha," I said.

"Aven," said Mom. "I hope you'll be supportive and understanding if one of your teammates becomes the captain."

"Of course I will," I said, secretly smirking because I knew that wouldn't be necessary. How could Dad choose anyone but me?

After dinner, Mom, Dad, and Great-grandma drank coffee out on the porch while I showed Great-grandma some of my best soccer moves. I dribbled around our grassy yard, feinting left and right in front of imaginary players.

"I like how you did that *stepover*," called Dad from the porch. "Maybe you could teach that to the rest of the girls tomorrow."

I stopped with my foot on top of the soccer ball, breathing hard from the exercise. I frowned a little because I kind of liked being the only girl on the team who could do that move.

Dad stared at me. "Do you have a problem with that, Aven?" he asked.

I shook my head. "No," I said. "No problem at all." But actually, I kind of did have a problem with it. Because if everyone could do the stepover as well as I could, then maybe I wouldn't be the best player on the team anymore.

Chapter 5

Toot Wars

By the next practice, I was so ready to show Dad that I, Aven Laura Green, was the best soccer player on the team. He'd better be wearing an extra pair of socks, because I was going to knock his first pair right off!

"Today I want you all to think of how you can encourage one another," said Coach Dad to all of us out on the field.

"You mean like saying nice things?" asked Lexi, wiping her nose.

Coach Dad nodded. "Yes, nice encouraging things."

"What does that mean exactly?" asked Ana.

Coach Dad looked around at each of us. "Have any of you really thought about what the word *encourage* means?"

We all shook our heads, because why would anyone care to think about something like that?

"Well," said Coach Dad. "What does it sound like?"

"It sounds like *encourage*," said Stacy. "En-cour-age."

"That kind of sounds like *porridge*," said Emily. "You know, from *Goldilocks and the Three Bears*." She squinted her eyes. "What even is porridge, anyway?"

"I think it's like oatmeal," I said.

"Nah," said Kayla. "I think it's pudding."

Coach Dad frowned. "Never mind about porridge," he said. "What about the word *courage*? Do you think it sounds like the word *courage*?"

We nodded our heads. "And also the word *en*," said Stacy.

"Right," said Coach Dad. "But let's go back to courage. What does *courage* mean?"

"Being brave," I said.

"Good, Aven," said Coach Dad. "Courage means bravery. And so *encourage* actually means putting courage, or bravery, into someone. It means doing and saying things that make your teammates feel braver."

Coach Dad seemed to think we all got the point, so we did the hand-and-foot stack before running out to the field, where I took my position as *striker*. Striker, in my opinion, was the most important position on the field. That's because the striker played near the goal and got to make the most goals. Lexi, the goalie, didn't stand a chance against me.

Sujata and Kayla took their positions as *midfielders*. The midfielders played in the middle of the field. Their job was to block the team from getting their ball to our side and also to get the ball to me as often as possible, so I could score a goal.

When Sujata passed the ball to me, I turned to kick it into the goal. Suddenly there was a loud explosion out on the field, followed by a terrible smell. I stumbled over the ball. Someone had used the toot decoy, and we were never ever supposed to use the toot decoy during practice!

Emily stole the ball from me and kicked it into the net, right past Lexi. Then Emily pumped her fist in the air and cried out, "Yes! Goal for me!"

"Not fair!" I cried back. "You used an illegal toot decoy!"

"Did not!" cried Emily.

"Did too!" I cried. "I smelled it."

Emily crossed her arms and tapped her foot on the grass. "Whoever smelt it dealt it," she said, grinning.

I was shocked, people, *shocked*. "I would never!" I insisted. We had all agreed—we save the toot decoy for games, not practice. "Whoever denied it supplied it!"

"Whoever disputed it tooted it!" said Emily.

"Whoever blamed it flamed it!" I said right back.

"If you point your finger, your butt's the singer," said Emily, pointing her finger right at me.

"Then that's you!" I said. "Because I don't even have a finger! And I heard it coming right from you—a giant explosion that nearly made my ears burst!"

"Yeah, well . . ." Emily narrowed her eyes at me, thinking. By now, all the other girls were gathering around us. "Whoever heard it turd it!"

"That doesn't even make sense," I said.

"Come on, you guys," said Kayla, putting her arms around the two of us. "We shouldn't fight. We should be working together."

I looked to Coach Dad, but he was just standing off to the side watching us. "Dad!" I whined. "Emily's not playing fair. I would've scored a goal if she hadn't used the toot decoy."

"No, it was Aven," said Emily.

"You girls work it out," Coach Dad said, which really wasn't helpful.

"It probably wasn't either of you," said Kayla, motioning her eyes toward Lexi. "And anyway, we're wasting valuable practice time. Now just say sorry, and let's get back to practice."

"Sorry," I grumbled, and I didn't even add "Toot Face" like I kind of wanted to.

"Sorry," Emily grumbled back.

Coach Dad nodded. "Good," he said. "Good job." But he was looking at Kayla, not me. All she'd done was tell me and Emily to say sorry, but Dad seemed really impressed about it for some reason. I knew I'd have to play extra hard for the rest of practice to show him I was still the best player on the team.

Chapter 6

Putting the Courage in Encourage

The next evening at practice, I decided to take Dad's advice and *encourage* my teammates. I was going to put some bravery and courage into them if it was the last thing I did, starting with our warm-up exercises.

"Move faster!" I shouted while we jogged around the field.

"Dribble better!" I cried while we dribbled across the field.

"Come on, Stacy!" I screamed while we did some sit-ups. "Stop being a wimp! Be brave!"

"Stop being so scared, Sujata!" I yelled while we did our free kicks. "Have some courage and kick that ball hard!"

When Kayla saw how scared Sujata was acting about kicking the ball past Lexi into the net, she went over and worked with her. As a matter of fact, she spent so much time working with Sujata that she didn't even have time to show off her own soccer skills. That meant more time for me to show Coach Dad that I was the best choice for soccer captain.

"Be brave!" I yelled at my teammates. "Move your butts!"

I glanced at Coach Dad, and he frowned at me. Was I not yelling loud enough?

"You're being a bit bossy, Aven," he said. "Don't you think?"

"But the captain is the boss, so I'm acting like a captain," I said.

"The captain is not *the* boss," he said. "Didn't you listen to anything I said when I explained what the captain does? How she encourages her teammates?"

"That's exactly what I'm doing, Dad," I said. "I just encouraged them all to move their butts."

Coach Dad's frown got even more frowny. "No, you *ordered* them to move their butts. Why don't you try complimenting them when they accomplish something and helping them when they have trouble? That would be a better way to encourage them."

I shrugged. "Okay," I said.

Then Coach Dad walked over to where

Kayla and Sujata were working together and watched them for a long time before calling me over. "Aven," he said, "Kayla's been trying to show Sujata how to do the stepover, but you're so good at it, we thought you might like to show her." He grinned. "You know, help her out, like we just talked about."

I gulped. Coach Dad wanted me to give away one of my best secrets. If I showed Sujata, then Kayla would see, too, and then Kayla could be almost as good as I was.

"I think I pulled a muscle," I said, leaning on one leg. "I can't do it right now."

Coach Dad frowned at me again. "But you were just kicking the ball around without any problems," he said.

"Fine," I said, and then I quickly showed Sujata how to do the stepover, but I made sure to do it not nearly as well as normal so that Kayla and Sujata couldn't steal my secrets. "And that's how you do it," I said, finishing up the move.

When I looked around at the three of them, I noticed they were all giving me dirty looks, especially Coach Dad. "Thanks for your help, Aven," he said, but it didn't sound like he was very grateful.

"That wasn't very helpful at all," said Kayla, crossing her arms.

Sujata shrugged. "That's okay," she said. "I'll just do it how Kayla showed me."

I smiled and nodded because that was definitely best for everyone.

Chapter 7

A Soccer Ball
Right to the Chest

After practice, Dad clapped his hands and called us all together. It was time to make the big announcement! I stood up straight and tall, ready to lead my team through thick and thin, through good times and bad times, through wins and losses (but mostly wins).

"You've all done such a great job," said Dad. "I'm so impressed with the progress the new players have made." He looked at Sujata.

"And Sujata, you've picked up soccer faster than anyone I've ever seen."

Sujata blushed and smiled. "Thank you, Coach Green," she said. "Kayla has been really helpful."

Dad looked at Kayla and nodded. "I know she has been," he said. "I've noticed how much time she's spent working with you, making sure you know all the rules and most important moves. She's also made sure the new players have been included as much as possible in every activity." Dad smiled at Kayla, and she smiled back. I didn't know why, but I was starting to get a sick feeling in my stomach.

"Kayla has been so helpful and supportive of the new players," said Dad. "She's acted like a real leader. She's also been a good example

of sportsmanship. And that's why she's going to be your new captain!"

Everyone clapped. Sujata threw her arms around Kayla and hugged her. Emily put an arm around Kayla and congratulated her too. Then Kayla looked at me with big eyes. She was waiting for me to say something, but I couldn't because my throat was all closed up and my eyes were getting hot. I just looked down at the ground, trying not to cry.

I didn't even want to do our hand-and-foot stack at the end of practice, so I guess it was really just a hand stack without my participation. Then everyone left, one by one, but Dad and I stayed out on the field together while Dad collected all the soccer stuff. "You okay, Aven?" he asked.

Again, I stared down at the field, trying not to cry. A nod was all I could do.

He walked to me and put a hand on my shoulder. "Are you upset?" he asked.

I shook my head, even though I felt very upset. "I'm okay," I whispered.

"You don't look okay," said Dad. "Is it about the captain?"

I finally looked up at him. "I thought you were going to make me the captain," I said. "I'm the best at the stepover, and no one else can even do the top secret booty trap. I've tried to be a good leader and tell the other girls what to do, but some of them don't even listen to me!"

"Aven," Dad said, his hands now on both my shoulders. He looked down at me very seriously. "Being the team captain isn't about bossing the other girls around and showing off your soccer skills. You *do* have great soccer skills. You *are* one of the best players on the team."

"Then why didn't you make me the captain, Dad?" I asked, a tear finally breaking loose and running down my cheek.

"Because being the captain is about being a leader. And the best leader leads by example, not by ordering others around. I feel like you have a lot to learn about teamwork still, Aven. In soccer, you seem to think only about how you can really shine. But you need to think about how you can help your whole team to shine. Understand?"

I nodded, but my stomach felt sicker than ever.

Dad sighed. "Aven," he said. "Just the fact that you're not happy for Kayla is a good example of why you shouldn't be the captain."

He stared down at me, his eyebrows drawn together. "I stand by my decision."

And that last thing he said was like a soccer ball hit me right in the chest at lightning speed, breaking my heart all up into a million little pieces.

Chapter 8

Quitting the Team

I was quiet all the way home, even though Dad kept trying to talk to me about all kinds of stuff. "You want to watch a movie together tonight?" he asked, but I didn't answer. "Maybe we could play a game. How about that one with the food crown? I'm going to beat you at that one of these days."

I still didn't answer. I just stared out the window, trying not to cry. Couldn't he see that I was giving him the silent treatment?

When we got home, I ran out of the car and stayed in my room, snuggling President Ollama on my bed, but even the president couldn't make me feel better. At one point, I heard Mom and Dad talking softly, and I peeked out my door and tried to spy on their conversation. Mom noticed me spying on them and told me it was time for dinner, so I finally left my room and walked to the table, slumping down in my chair with a great big sigh.

Mom placed a plate of meatloaf and mashed potatoes in front of me, but I wasn't hungry. I just stared at my plate.

"Aven and I were thinking we'd play that food crown game after dinner," said Dad, chewing his meatloaf like nothing at all was wrong. "Maybe we could do it for dessert. I think we have some strawberries in the fridge."

"That sounds like fun," said Mom.

"I don't want to play the food game," I muttered.

"Well, then, we could play another game," said Mom. "Or we could watch something. I heard there's a new episode of *Jake's Rake Cake Snake Bake*. Apparently, they're allowing the bakers to use shovels and pickaxes now."

"I don't want to watch anything," I grumbled.

Mom nodded. "Okay, then," she said. "I guess you probably should get to bed early. You have a long day tomorrow with school and soccer practice right after. I'm sure you'll feel better after a good night's rest."

"I won't be going to soccer practice tomorrow," I said, staring at my meatloaf.

Dad dropped his fork, and it made a loud clang against his plate. "What are you talking about, Aven?" he asked.

Tears stung my eyes. "I won't be going," I said in a shaky voice, "because I'm quitting the team!" And with that I jumped up and ran away from the table.

Chapter 9

The Best Heart

I'd never felt so low in my life. Even when I couldn't find Smitty. Even when my friends kicked me off the baking team. Even when I thought I couldn't learn to play an instrument, I didn't feel this low. I was as low as Earth's core. Trust me—I learned all about Earth's layers in school, and it doesn't get any lower than that!

My own dad didn't think I was good enough to be the team captain. What would

Mom say when she found out? Would she be mad at him for being so mean to me? Or worse, would she agree with him? I felt sick as I snuggled President Ollama.

Someone knocked softly on my door. I stayed quiet, pretending I wasn't home. Then the door slowly opened, and Mom peeked her head in. "Can I come in, honey?" she asked.

I shrugged but didn't say anything, so Mom came in and sat down on the bed next to me. I sat up and hung my head, staring at my carpet.

"I'd love to know what's going on in that red head of yours," she said. "I'm sure Dad would too."

I sniffled. "Dad already knows what's going on in my red head," I said. "He's the one who put all these bad thoughts in there."

"Really?" said Mom. "What did he do?"

I finally looked up at her. "He made Kayla captain instead of me, his own daughter!"

Mom nodded thoughtfully. "Yes, I know."

"So what do you think of that?" I demanded.

She tilted her head and put her arm around me, a sad look on her face. "He explained his choice to me, and I agree with him that it was the right one."

My mouth dropped open. So not only did my own father think I wasn't good enough to be captain, but my own mother agreed with him. I was wrong—it *was* possible to feel lower than Earth's core.

"How can you say such a thing?" I asked. "Don't you guys love me?"

"Oh, honey," Mom said, squeezing her arms around me. "We love you more than anything in this whole wide world. And sometimes, we love you so much that we have to make really hard choices that can make you mad at us.

"I don't understand," I said. "Why would you want me to be mad at you?"

"We don't want you to be mad at us, Aven. But sometimes the best thing for you isn't the thing that makes you the happiest."

"How can this be best for me?" I said.

"Because it's so much more important that you learn and grow from this experience," she said. "We're very concerned about the kind of person you'll become, and we felt this would be best for your heart."

"But he *broke* my heart," I said, tears filling my eyes. "He broke it up into a million pieces."

Mom hugged me tighter. "It was such a hard decision for him," she said. "But the most important thing to us is making sure we do what we can to help you grow up to be the best person you can be. You may feel sad about it now, but one day you'll look back, and I think you'll understand. You'll be grateful Dad didn't make you captain when you still had so much to learn about being a leader and a team player. Remember the baking competition?"

I nodded. Of course I remembered. I'd tried to force everyone to do things my way, and that hadn't turned out well at all.

"Even though you didn't get your way with the baking competition, you learned a lot about supporting a team, didn't you?" said Mom.

I nodded again. I had been pretty bossy during the baking competition. It hadn't made my friends very happy, and it hadn't made me happy either.

"Listen," said Mom. "Dad and I know you're a natural leader, Aven, but we want you to be the best leader you can be. Sometimes that means supporting other leaders. So will you support Kayla as the captain? Or will you quit the sport you love?"

I stared down at my carpet, not sure how to answer that question. I was quiet a long time.

"Aven," Mom finally said, tilting my chin up with her hand so I was looking at her. "I know that when you put your mind to something and work really hard to accomplish your goals, you can be the best at just about anything. That's all fine, but that's not what's most important to Dad and me." She took her hand from my chin and pressed it to the center of my chest. "What's most important to us is that you have the best *heart.*"

Chapter 10

The Flamethrower Story

I had some really serious soul-searching to do, so I went in the backyard to kick around the soccer ball as the sun began to set. I hoped that would help me find my soul. After kicking the ball a few times, I heard a familiar voice shout my name. I looked up and saw Great-grandma standing on the back porch.

"Come sit with me awhile, my dear," Great-grandma said, sitting down in a lawn chair and patting the one next to her.

I kicked the ball across the yard into a bush. Then I walked up the wooden porch steps, slumping my shoulders as much as possible, and flopped down into the chair next to her. "Hi, Grandma," I said, my voice sad and low.

"What's the matter, honey?" Great-grandma asked.

I sighed, lifting my shoulders up and slumping them down even further. "I'm just sad," I said. "Dad doesn't think very highly of me, Grandma."

Her old face was filled with shock. "What?" she asked.

I nodded. "That's right. He doesn't want me to be soccer captain."

Great-grandma smiled. "Oh, Aven," she said. "I happen to know that your dad thinks you're the best person he's ever met."

"Then how could he not make me soccer captain?" I asked.

Great-grandma scratched her head. "You want to hear a story?" she asked.

"Only if it's a story about Dad changing his mind and making me soccer captain," I said.

Great-grandma laughed. "It's a better story than that," she said, and I got the feeling she was going to tell it to me no matter what I wanted. Great-grandma cleared her throat. "Once, when your dad was your age, he wanted a flamethrower."

My ears perked up, and I gave Great-grandma my full attention because this story was off to a really good start.

"Of course his parents wouldn't let him get one," she said. "So what does he do?" She chuckled. "He comes to Grandma, of course. He begged me for a flamethrower, so I asked him why he wanted one so badly. And do you know what he told me?"

I shook my head, absolutely fascinated by this story, people. Fascinated.

"He said there was a snake living under his front porch," she said. "And his parents wouldn't do anything about it. They didn't care that there was a snake under there, but your dad was positively terrified of this snake,

so he decided burning it out with a flame-thrower was the only solution. He wanted a flamethrower so badly, he cried."

"So did you get him one?" I asked.

Great-grandma's mouth dropped open. "Of course not! If I'd gotten him a flame-thrower, he'd have burned the whole house down!"

"What did you do then?" I asked.

"I stormed right over to the house, got a rake, and dragged that snake out from under there," she said. "It was just a harmless little ringneck snake. I picked it up with my bare hands to show him."

"With your bare hands?" I said. "You're brave, Grandma."

"Yes, I am," she said. "But it didn't take much bravery to catch that snake, because I wasn't scared. Your dad showed some brav-ery, though, when he touched it, because he was terrified of that snake. Positively terrified."

"He touched it?" I asked.

"Yep," said Great-grandma. "And then we walked it out to the woods and let it go."

"That was an awesome story, Grandma," I said. "Why'd you tell it to me?"

"Because, Aven…" Great-grandma frown-ned. She scratched her gray head. And shifted in her seat. "Huh," she said. "Why *did* I tell you that story?" Then she lifted her wrinkly finger in the air. "Oh, right!" she declared. "Because sometimes the people who love you don't give you what you want because they know it's not good for you and could even burn the house down."

"That's just what Mom said, except for the house-burning-down thing," I said, kicking my legs and staring down at the porch.

"It's the truth," said Great-grandma, then her face lit up. "Oh, now look who's here!"

I looked up and there was Kayla, standing in the grass in the middle of my backyard.

Chapter 11

The Best Choice

"Well, if it isn't one of your very best friends," said Great-grandma.

Kayla walked up the porch steps and gave Great-grandma a hug. "Hi, Mrs. Jackson," she said.

"Nice to see you, Kayla," said Great-grandma. Then Great-grandma hugged me and whispered, "Think about what I said," before going back inside the house, leaving me and Kayla on the porch alone.

Kayla stood in front of me all quiet and shy, which wasn't like her at all. "Hi," she finally said softly.

"Hi," I said back.

We were quiet a long time until Kayla finally said, "I heard you want to quit the team."

I shrugged. That is what I'd wanted, but now I wasn't feeling so sure. "I don't know," I said. "I'm still deciding."

"Can I help you make your decision?" asked Kayla.

"Sure," I said. I could definitely use the help, because this was a very confusing decision to make.

"Okay," said Kayla, taking a big breath. "I don't think you should quit the team, and here's why: One." Kayla held up a finger.

"You're a really good player, so our team won't be as good without you. Two." Kayla held up two fingers. "You'll miss out on the pizza party, ice cream party, ice pops after practice, and all the hand-and-foot stacks. And three." Kayla held up three fingers. "It will make me really sad, because I'll miss you."

I looked down at the porch because I felt like crying again all of a sudden. "I'll miss you too," I said softly.

"Maybe we could play a game of one-on-one to help you decide," said Kayla. She narrowed her eyes at me. "I bet you can't beat me."

I looked up at her and grinned. "I bet I can."

"I bet I'll destroy you," said Kayla.

"I bet you'll go down in flames," I said, running for the soccer ball in the bush. I kicked it out.

Kayla was already right behind me in her ready soccer stance. "That bush is the goal for me, and that tree is the goal for you," she said. "Five goals to win."

And then we played one-on-one until I had five goals and Kayla only had four. We stood,

staring at each other, breathing hard from running around so much. "You win," said Kayla. "Good game."

"Good game," I agreed.

Kayla took a few more breaths and then smiled. "You're really a great soccer player, Aven."

I smiled back. "So are you," I said.

"Not as good as you, though," said Kayla. "Have you made up your mind yet?"

Before I could answer her, Mom stepped out onto the porch, her hands on her hips. "You girls want some ice cream?" she asked.

"Yeah," cried Kayla, running inside. I stood on the grass, the soccer ball under my foot, finishing up the last of my soul-searching. I felt a lot better than I had just a little while ago, and not just because of Great-grandma's awesome flamethrower story, but because of Kayla too.

I hadn't acted happy for Kayla for being made team captain. I didn't congratulate her, and I hadn't been nice at all. But she still came over here to see me and ask me to stay on the team.

Maybe that was what Dad meant when he said the team captain needed to support and encourage her teammates. Maybe that was what he'd meant about putting courage into someone. I'd been feeling pretty scared of going back to practice after the way I'd acted, but now I was feeling like I could face my team again.

"Aren't you coming, Aven?" Kayla asked, standing on the porch again.

I looked up at her. "Kayla," I said. "I just want to tell you congratulations on being made team captain."

She beamed at me. "Thank you, Aven."

I smiled and told her, "Dad made a really good choice."

Chapter 12

Unquitting the Team

After school the next day, I got home and put on my soccer gear. When I walked out into the living room, Dad looked me over. "Oh, are you coming with me?" he asked.

I looked down at the carpet. "If that's okay with you," I said.

Dad put an arm around my shoulders and squeezed. "It's definitely okay with me," he said.

I smiled up at him. "Then I'd like to unquit the team if you'll hire me back."

Dad grinned. "You're hired, Sheebs."

As we drove to practice, Dad even put on the "Getting Pumped for Soccer" playlist, but as we pulled into the parking lot at the field, my stomach felt sick. I hoped my teammates weren't mad at me for the way I acted.

When Kayla and Sujata saw our car pull in, they ran over to us with big smiles. "Oh, yay!" said Kayla. "You're here!"

And you know what? They seemed like they were really happy to see me.

When we jogged around the field, I didn't yell at anyone. I just focused on doing my best, and when Sujata started falling back, I slowed down and jogged with her so she wouldn't feel bad about being slow. When we did sit-ups, I didn't scream at anyone to do more. I just did as many as I could and then told the others they did a good job. And when

we dribbled, I showed Ana how to control the ball better by using the inside of her foot instead of the front.

When practice was over, Coach Dad blew his whistle and called us all around. "Tomorrow we have our first big game," he said. "Whether we win or lose, I want you to know I'm so proud of how well you're all doing." He grinned at Sujata and Ana. "Especially the new girls. You're both learning so much." Then he looked around at all of us. "Now, is there anything anyone wants to discuss or any special practice requests before tomorrow?"

Everyone stayed quiet, but I cleared my throat. "I have something I'd like to discuss," I said.

"Yes, Aven?" said Coach Dad.

I walked up next to him, faced my team, and put my foot on the soccer ball. I cleared my throat again. "I think everyone could do a better stepover," I said. "You just need to know this one little trick."

Then I showed them my secret trick for doing the stepover. Because it was super cool that I could do a really good stepover, but if we could all do it, then our team would really shine.

Chapter 13

Still Top Secret

The next day, just before the big game, we all wished the other team good luck to show our excellent sportsmanship. Then we did our special hand-and-foot stack to pump ourselves up.

We all took our positions on the field, and the referee blew the whistle to start the game. The other team scored the first goal, blowing the ball right past Lexi. They were really good, and I worried we might not beat them.

Back and forth it went like this through-
out the whole game: goal for them, goal for
us, goal for them, goal for us.

When we were down by one and time was
running out, Kayla kicked the ball to me. I
turned and saw that I could probably take a
shot past the other team's goalie, but I also
realized that Sujata hadn't scored a goal the
whole game. I looked at her, and she was in
her ready stance in case I kicked the ball to
her. She was also wide open.

Instead of taking the shot for myself, I decided to kick the ball to Sujata in the hopes that she would be able to score at least one goal during her first big game. She stopped the ball with her foot and turned. Then she took a deep breath, her face filled with worry as she faced the goalie.

"No more Mister Nice Sujata!" I cried, reminding her to kick that ball as hard as she could at the goal.

She pulled her foot back and kicked that

ball as hard as I'd ever seen. The other team's goalie jumped for the ball and missed. Sujata scored the goal to tie the game!

Sujata and I ran to each other and jumped up and down in a big, excited hug. I felt so happy that I'd kicked the ball to Sujata instead of taking another goal for myself.

Now we were tied with only a couple of minutes left in the game. We all went back to our positions. I bounced from foot to foot, ready to end this game the best I could. And I knew, whether we won or lost, I would feel good about the day and how hard our team had tried.

Right away, Kayla was able to steal the ball from the other team. Then she kicked the ball to me, but she kicked it too high. It went way up in the air. A girl on the other team moved next to me, preparing to steal the ball when it came down. Down, down, down it came, bouncing on the ground right between us, but when the girl moved in to steal it, I cried out, "Not today!" I moved my leg over the ball, so that when it bounced up, it hit my butt. Top secret booty trap to the rescue! I dribbled the ball toward the goal and kicked. In it went! Final goal of the day to break the tie. We won!

All my friends ran around me, hugging and cheering. Top secret booty trap saved the day! And I could still call it top secret since I hadn't yet taught it to my teammates. I had to have *one* special secret for myself.

Chapter 14

The Sticker Kickers

"Girls, I'm so proud of all of you," said Coach Dad. "And not because you won. You all acted kind and respectful out there. You supported one another. And you showed fantastic sportsmanship." Dad grinned. "Plus, you really kicked some butt."

We all jumped up and down and cheered for ourselves. Because we were awesome.

"I'm very impressed with our new players' growth," continued Coach Dad. "Sujata, your progress is astounding. That goal you made was spectacular." Coach Dad glanced at me and winked.

Sujata blushed while everyone patted her on the back. "Thank you," she said. "I couldn't have learned so much without my friends' help."

"And there's another player who has shown tremendous growth as well," said Coach Dad. "Rather than focusing on how she can be the best player, she's been focusing on how she can be the best team player. I've noticed all her efforts, and so I would like to make this girl the vice captain."

"Oh, is that like the vice president?" asked Ana.

"Yes," said Dad. "Just like the vice president supports the president, the vice captain supports the captain."

"And also the vice president becomes president if the president kicks the bucket," said Lexi.

"Uh," stuttered Coach Dad. "Right. But we don't have to worry about the captain kicking the bucket."

"That's right," I said. "Kayla is very healthy. I've even seen her eat broccoli before."

"Yep," said Kayla. "And I brush my teeth every day."

"But really you never know," said Emily, shrugging. "You could get struck by lightning or sucked up in a tornado or something."

Coach Dad got that confused look again, like he forgot what he was even talking about. "No, no, no," he said, shaking his head. "No one's getting struck by lightning or getting sucked up in a tornado. We're losing focus again. Anyway, the vice captain steps in wherever and whenever the captain needs her. She has very important responsibilities. She is a wonderful assistant—kind and caring and supportive."

I prepared myself for Dad to name a girl. I would have the biggest smile for her. I would cheer for her louder than anyone else. Maybe I could even make her a special "Congratulations" card with my new soccer stickers. I would make up for how I had acted when Kayla was made captain.

"And that girl is . . ." Coach Dad said. Then he looked at me. "That girl is Aven."

At first I didn't think I'd heard Coach Dad right, but there wasn't anyone else on the team whose name sounded like mine. So he must've said my name! "Me?" I asked just to be sure.

Coach Dad grinned. "Yes, you, Aven," he said.

I was so surprised I could barely speak. My teammates all gathered around and hugged me and told me they were happy for me. Because the Sticker Kickers had great sportsmanship, and now I did too.

Chapter 15

Time for a Break

To celebrate finishing our first game, our parents surprised us with a big ice cream sundae bar out on the field—there were all kinds of sprinkles, syrups, whipped cream, and even bright red cherries. I helped Kayla pick all of her toppings because I was a really good assistant.

"Just think," Kayla whispered to me while we sat in the grass eating our ice cream together. "If you'd quit the team, you couldn't be here with us right now eating ice cream."

Boy, was Kayla right. The ice cream wasn't all I'd have missed out on, though. I'd have missed out on the game today. I'd have missed out on teaching everyone how to do the stepover. I'd have missed out on seeing Sujata make her first goal. I'd have missed out on doing the top secret booty trap. I'd have missed out on being vice captain, though that wasn't the most important thing. If I'd quit, I'd just be sitting at home hanging out with President Ollama. That sounded really boring.

I went to take a big bite of ice cream with whipped cream on top, and Kayla reached over and bumped my spoon so that whipped cream went on my nose. All the girls giggled, so I flung my whole spoonful of ice cream at Kayla and it landed in her hair. Then she flung a spoonful at me, but I have lightning-quick reflexes and ducked. The ice cream flew over my head and landed in Lexi's lap.

The next thing we knew, ice cream was flying everywhere. Girls ran around in circles screaming, chocolate and sprinkles dripping from their hair, whipped cream all over their arms, cherries sticking out of their ears.

It was chaos, people. Chaos! A big bite even landed right on Coach Dad's shoulder. It was one of the funniest things that had ever happened to me!

On the way home in the car, I was so tired and full of sugar (and also covered in sugar) that I almost fell asleep. "You look sleepy, Sheebs," Dad said.

"I think an early bedtime is in order," added Mom.

"I feel like I could sleep for a month," I said, leaning my head against the window.

"You've been awfully busy lately," said Mom. "Solving mysteries, entering baking competitions, practicing the guitar, and lots of soccer. I think we could all use a break."

"What kind of break?" I asked.

"Well, how about a vacation?" she said to Dad and me.

"A vacation?" I said. "Where?"

Mom shrugged. "I don't know. We could decide together."

"I could certainly use a vacation," said Dad.

"A vacation sounds like so much fun," I said. If we were going to go on a vacation, then I would vacation harder than anyone had ever vacationed before.

Watch out, world! Here comes Aven Green Vacation Machine!

Aven's Soccer Words

flip-flap: a move used to fool a defensive player into thinking the offensive player (player who has the ball) is going to move in a direction they do not intend to; feint

feint: see flip-flap; not to be confused with instantly going to sleep and falling to the ground

cleat: a shoe with bumps on the sole to prevent slipping

shin: a chunk of your leg; not to be confused with chin, a chunk of your face

sportsmanship: fair and respectful treatment toward others in sports

stepover: an offensive soccer move for getting around a defender

striker: a forward; the closest player to the opponent's goal, largely responsible for scoring goals

midfielder: a soccer position between the team's defenders and forwards

Dusti Bowling

grew up in Scottsdale, Arizona, where, as her family will tell you, she always had her nose in a book. Dusti holds a Bachelor of Psychology and a Master of Education, but she eventually realized her true passion was writing. She is the author of *Insignificant Events in the Life of a Cactus* and *24 Hours in Nowhere*. She lives in Arizona with her husband, three daughters, a dozen tarantulas, too many scorpions, a gopher snake named Burrito, and a cockatiel named Cilantro.

Aven Green can do just about anything!

She is great
at solving
mysteries in

Aven Green
SLEUTHING MACHINE

She is an
expert baker in

Aven Green
BAKING MACHINE

She is a professional
musician in

Aven Green
MUSIC MACHINE

She is
a talented player in

Aven Green
SOCCER MACHINE